# Filly Girls

## CHASING THE DREAM

To Weston
Dream Big

# Filly Girls

## CHASING THE DREAM

### TOGETHER FOREVER ALWAYS

By Sarah Voskamp

Filly Girls Chasing the Dream
© 2010 Sarah Voskamp. All rights reserved.

Published in the USA by:
Boutique of Quality Books Publishing Company
www.boutiqueofqualitybooks.com

Printed in the United States of America
ISBN 978-0-9828689-7-3

Library of Congress Control Number: 2010940953

Book & cover design by Darlene Swanson • www.van-garde.com
Illustrations by Steve McGinnis • www.digraphics.info

Printed by SBI
Chelsea, MI USA
1/26/11 - 2/8/11
324425

# *Dedication*

I dedicate this story to my dad who helped me along the way, my mom who encourages me to keep going, my friends Ally and Ansley who inspired me, my book and my characters, and also my older brothers who always say, "Wow, you are doing my essays!"

# Chapter 1

December 25th is a day I will always remember. It was on that day a miracle happened for me. You are probably thinking that I'm talking about the miracle of Christmas. Well there is that, but this one was different, and my whole life changed. From that day forward, my life as a horseback riding, twelve-year-old girl would turn out to be much more meaningful. Life as I knew it would never be the same.

That morning, when I woke up from a surprisingly normal dream, I stretched and thought, *Today is the day I have been waiting*

*for since the beginning of January. Christmas!!*
I jumped out of bed, scurried down the stairs,
and glimpsed quickly in my stocking, but
before I could see anything I heard my mother
wake up from a blissful sleep. I can always tell
when she's had a good or bad night's rest. Not
wanting to get caught peeking at my presents,
I ran as fast as I could back up the stairs to my
room and jumped on my bed. Ouch! I missed
the bed and hit the floor because I didn't jump
far enough. I have to be a little more careful
next time.

The loud bang woke up everyone in the
house—which wasn't too many because I am
an only child—so we decided to go downstairs
and open some gifts. Yeah! As we do every
Christmas, we opened them in order, one by
one, and Mom got to go first. I was so excited
I could hardly wait for my turn, but it was so
worth the wait because I got the best gifts
ever—everything that was on my list and much
more! I received bunches of clothes and gift

cards and most exciting of all, a brand new show outfit, show helmet, chaps, and leather boots! What a great Christmas it was turning out to be.

After our gifts were opened and we were full from the delicious Christmas morning breakfast that my mom made, my best friends Sandra and Felicity called and asked if I wanted to go on a Christmas trail ride. I, of course, said "Yes!" I love to ride and I have been riding since I was about four. Mom and Dad saw how much I loved horses so they let me take lessons and I have been riding ever since.

I quickly grabbed my riding gear out of the closet, threw on my jacket, and zoomed out the door. I ran as fast as I could over to my neighbors to borrow a horse for the ride like I always do. When I arrived at their barn and opened the big doors I realized something was different. I backed up a little and saw a big blue ribbon draped across several stalls. *That's weird* I thought. As I looked closer I spotted a big tag that said,

"Merry Christmas, Ellie!
XOXOXO
Ho Ho Ho!
Love, Mom and Dad"

I couldn't believe it so I turned back towards the doors and saw Mom and Dad peeking inside the barn with smiles beaming from ear to ear. They were giggling and laughing as they walked inside and said, "Go on, Honey, look around."

I walked towards the back of the barn where the big blue ribbon was wrapped across four stalls. I couldn't believe what I saw next. Poking out of one of the stalls was a black muzzle. OMG, now I really couldn't believe it! For Christmas my parents had given me several stalls in the barn *and* a horse of my very own. This was the best gift anyone could get! Ever!

I walked over to the stall and looked into the most beautiful face I have ever seen. There she was—a beautiful filly with a dark brown coat and a black muzzle, mane and tail. A million thoughts raced through my head all at once: *Just wait until I tell my friends. They'll freak out!* Wait, *I'm Freaking out!*

As I walked closer to the stall to meet my new filly for the first time, I thought *What am I going to name her?* I considered several different names—I thought of Molly, Lightening, and even Bella, but none of them were quite right. Then I heard my next door neighbor say, "It's a miracle! I bet Ellie never thought something like this would ever happen to her."

"PERFECT!" I screamed. "Miracle! That's what I'm going to name her." Now THAT name fit perfectly because miraculous was just what this felt like to me. I glanced over to see Sandra and Felicity standing with their mouths wide open. Apparently it felt miraculous to them, too. I couldn't help but giggle. Almost in a blur, I hugged and thanked my parents, grabbed my friends to come check out my new horse, then saddled and bridled Miracle for the trail ride.

In the barn, there was other new stuff besides Miracle. I got a new saddle blanket, a new saddle, new bridle, and all new grooming stuff too !! When I showed Felicity and Sandra and told them about everything else I had gotten for Christmas, they said I was lucky and that their parents were frugal. This means they like to spend their money very carefully (or not at all). I still couldn't believe what a miracle Miracle was.

As we left on our trail ride, I felt like I was in a dream as Felicity and her horse Babe, Sandra and her horse Dream, and Miracle and I rode into Tree Hill Forest on the trail we always took. But this time I was on my very own horse.

We rode quite a while just chatting and having a great time, but for me it was the best ride I had ever taken because I had my very own Miracle.

When we returned to the barn we washed

and groomed our horses. Miracle especially liked the curry comb. As we groomed and chatted, we were so excited about Miracle and Christmas that we decided to have a slumber party that night so we could gossip about everything that had happened.  When we finished up in the barn we ran to ask our parents' permission and started planning our Christmas sleepover.

It really shouldn't be called a sleepover because we didn't sleep much at all. We were too excited about Christmas, the gifts we had gotten and of course about my Christmas Miracle.

When morning came, Felicity and Sandra fell asleep but I was still too excited so I decided to check my email and maybe grab some breakfast. When I saw my email I forgot all about breakfast because I got a note that said the happiest thing in the world:

*Hi Ellie,*

*We would like to invite you to the Georgia State Equestrian Show. Because of your riding experience you are able to compete in the English or Western Riding Division, whichever you prefer. If you place in the top five, you can proceed to the national competition. If you place in the top three at the national competition, you will qualify for the world competition. This is a big opportunity, and we would be honored for you to compete.*

I was so excited I ran upstairs and woke up Sandra and Felicity to share the news. They got so excited that they decided to check their emails too and saw that they had both received a similar email. We all screamed in happiness.

"Yea! Yea! Yea! Yea! Yea! Yea!"

None of us could believe it. We had been hoping for this, for like, forever. We continued to read the invitation and saw that it said that we had to go to Atlanta and be there in six weeks. It was signed "Robin Whayhuter." I knew I had heard Robin's name before, but it took me a moment to place it.

Then I remembered that she was my old trainer who had moved to Australia a few years ago. She had wanted to stay and help me continue improving as a rider, but she got married so she had to go.

"Is something wrong?" Sandra asked when she saw the strange look on my face.

"No, not really, I was just remembering where I heard that name before." Then I told my friends where I knew Robin from.

We were all so excited that we almost immediately started training for the show. The email instructed us to leave in six weeks from Friday and we had tons of stuff to do. So we ran to tell our families the big news and to ask our parents if we could attend and started to make our big plans.

Even though the show was not far from my home in Cumming, Georgia, we all decided to go early and Felicity, Sandra, and I were going to share a room next to our parents at a five-star hotel not far from the arena. After our parents made the reservations, we found out that our room would be #354, which was supposed to be a lucky room. We had heard that if you stayed there you would definitely win the show. So we were all really excited that it was our room, I just hoped it was true!

After all our plans were set, I decided to write a note back to Robin. It said:

*Hi, Robin,*

*Thank you so much for the invitation to the show. I will definitely be there. Sounds like so much fun. I can't wait! See ya there.*

*Sincerely,*
*Ellie Kerhage*

*P.S. I am staying in the lucky room!*

Sandra, Felicity and I all worked every hour we could to get ourselves and our horses ready for the show.  We were so tired at night that we didn't even talk much on the phone or watch any TV.  I think we shocked our parents. There was no way anyone else was going to win this competition but us!

I knew the competition at the show would be intense so it was hard to find me anywhere but the practice ring. I felt like I needed to be practicing day and night. In fact, if mom hadn't made me, I wouldn't have gotten much sleep in the weeks before the big day. I had to practice, practice, practice and take advantage of the six weeks before the show.

All I could do was eat, sleep, talk, or think about the show. Yet at night every nightmare or dream I had was about something random, never the show. It was like when I fell asleep I stopped thinking about the show or even winning. That was weird! Maybe it was a signal that the show was going to be good or maybe

I was going to be voted the best and be pinned # 1. I couldn't wait.

I was so focused on the show that I almost forgot that I had to take care of Miracle's stalls, replace her hay, and feed and groom her. Felicity and Sandra helped me so it didn't take very long, even though there were four stalls.

I wanted to hire people to help, but mom thought quite differently—she thought I should do it all by myself. She said it made me more responsible, but I decided to go with my idea about hiring people.

I thought Jeremy, a friend of mine, would be a good stall cleaner. I also needed a trainer, groomer, and maybe some other people, too. Soon, I would have a barn full of horses and trainers, and everything! I would make these extreme "Miracle" weeks. I was actually still in a state of disbelief. Was Miracle a real miracle? Well she was to me!

It turned out that Mom got her way and I ended up doing all the stuff myself. But that was okay because I knew that after I won the state, national and world championships I would have lots of people to help take care of all my horses. But I knew that Miracle would always be my favorite.

# Chapter 2

It was Thursday—the day before we were leaving for the show—and I had been packing and repacking all day. Every time I turned around I would pack something new. The fifth time I repacked my bag, I included a diary. I planned to write in it every day. When I told Felicity and Sandra about it, they decided to pack one also. I wanted to make sure I could remember every moment of the show!

Just as I was finally finished packing, I realized OMG, I had forgotten to pack my lucky ring that my great-grandma had given me when I was a baby. How dare I forget something so important! I ran to get it and stuffed it in my bag. I couldn't leave that behind or I would have no chance of winning. I am so glad I remembered it before we left because I don't think Mom and Dad would have been too thrilled to turn around and come back for it.

The night before we had to leave I wrote in my diary.

Dear Diary,

Today I went to school, and then to my riding lessons and worked with Miracle to get ready for the show. Then I went over and hung out with Sandra and Felicity for a while. Today was fun except for the school part. We leave tomorrow for the big horse show and I am so excited I don't think I will be able to sleep!

Ellie

Since we were leaving the next morning, I went to bed earlier than usual and tried to get at least a little sleep. It didn't work.

The next morning I jumped out of bed, got ready and rolled my suitcase to the car. I almost fainted it was so heavy! We pulled out of the driveway at 10:00 a.m. and I was sound asleep when we arrived in Atlanta a little less than an hour later.

My mother carried me into the hotel and tucked me in bed so I could continue resting. I was so disoriented that when I woke up and stretched I thought I would bang my head on the roof of the car.   Realizing we were already at the hotel, I said, "So we're here finally. I can win now."

My mom smiled and responded, "Not exactly. You still have five days until the show." I just mumbled at her and nodded as I realized all of the things I had to do before I could win.

First things first, I had to practice and get myself and Miracle familiar with the arena. I

was only allowed a half an hour each morning and a half an hour each late afternoon. I hoped that Miracle and I could do this with the limited time we had. But I had faith in us! Later that day at my assigned time, I walked to the arena to practice, practice, practice. The only problem was Miracle wouldn't move—that's right, I was here for a competition and my horse wouldn't move.  Great!  But after a little hard work, and a lot of coaxing, she started to feel comfortable and not frightened at all.

Now it was down to business. Miracle was a very good horse and it didn't take long before we had memorized the pattern by heart and all of the jumps we would have to ride in the show. I hoped my buddies would be able to memorize their patterns too.

Dear Diary,
It's Tuesday and we've been here since last Friday. I've been so busy practicing I haven't had much time to write. But the practice is paying off. Miracle got used to the pattern very quickly and she's a natural jumper. I memorized the pattern

for the show and my practice days are over. The show starts tomorrow!        Ellie

I hadn't written in my diary in a long time, but Tuesday was nearly over and it was my last practice day. After practice, I had to braid Miracle's tail and mane and groom her. That shouldn't have been hard but it was. As a matter of fact, it was extremely hard because Miracle wouldn't stand still for anything.  I think she was nervous, but we got through it. I can get through anything.

Sorry. I was thinking about myself—I caught myself in the act. Code Red.  What I meant to say was WE can get through anything, Miracle and I.

When I finished cleaning and perking Miracle up a bit, I roamed around town with Felicity and Sandra. We found this horse store that had this exquisite show outfit, saddle, and other cool horse gear. I begged Mom to get the stuff. She kept saying "no," but finally gave in. I really didn't need it because I had just received lots of new gear for Christmas, but I thought this outfit and saddle would help my chances of winning the show. Mom was always really cool when I needed her help with something really important.

When I got back to the hotel I saw Felicity's diary sitting out. I know I shouldn't have done it, but I peeked in and flipped to a page, and I couldn't help but read it. It said:

This is Felicity. I want to tell you who I have a crush on. This very special guy is . . . Jeremy. He is so cute and sweet. He is also the same guy Ellie wants as her stall cleaner. I love him. I can't help it. Don't tell ANYONE. FELICITY

I turned around and you would never guess who was there. Felicity! Uh-oh, spaghetti-o. What was I going to do?

I thought if I could explain everything, it would be okay. But I was way off. I was off by a mile, maybe even more. She was angry and said, "I'm not going to talk to you until after I win the show," and stomped off down the hotel hallway.

*Okay*, I thought a little boastfully, *I guess that'll be never*. But I really wondered how I was going to win if I knew she was mad at me and wouldn't talk to me ever again. I knew I would be distracted and I was worried. I had to try and make it right. She was, after all, one of my best friends. Then I remembered my lucky charm (my great-grandma's ring). It was the key to every success, whether it was trouble with a best friend or winning a horse show.

But then it was time for dinner so I didn't have a lot of time to think about what I was going to do to make it right with Felicity. My parents and I ate at the best place in town—Maggiano's—so I had food on my mind.

After dinner we went back to the hotel and watched a few movies. I fell asleep pretty early, about 9:00 p.m. I was really tired and the show was the next day, so I needed my sleep. *I'll figure out what to do about Felicity tomorrow.*

That evening my Mom and Dad met some of the other parents to enjoy "some grownup time" and that's when they found out the bad news, but decided not to tell us girls until the morning.

Totally unaware that my world was going to come crashing down in the morning, that night I dreamed about the show. I dreamed that Miracle, Dream, and Babe tied for first in the state competition and also at the national competition. Then, at the world competition, guess who was voted first place? It was a tie! Babe, Dream, and Miracle—again! Can you believe it was all three of us again? But that was just a dream and in reality, it would never happen. It could be really close, but it would never be an exact tie for first. Even if I wished really hard, which I did.

I woke up in the morning ready to participate in the competition…and win…but that's when I heard the bad news.

# Chapter 3

When I got out of bed, that is when my Mom told me, "Sweetie, one of the judges has died, so the show isn't going on."

I immediately felt bad for the judge and scared for what that meant for me. "What?" I screamed. "This can't happen! Today is the day, and the show has to go on! Okay, maybe not today, but it's going to happen, right? *Right*?"

All I heard was mumbling because my confused thoughts didn't let me hear the words. *This cannot be happening*, I thought. I had been waiting for this moment, and now the show had been canceled. I had to do something about this!

I had some serious thinking to do, so I went where I think the best—down at the stables, deep in the hay with my horse right next to me—and pondered the situation. Miracle whinnied, and I could tell she wanted to go for a ride.

Just as I was saddling up, Sandra and Felicity walked into the barn and I asked them to join me for a ride so we could talk together and figure out just what we were going to do. It couldn't end like this…it just couldn't!

Felicity didn't mention the diary incident; I was either forgiven or she had already forgotten about it. As we rode, all we could talk about was the show and how unfair it was that it had been canceled just like that. They couldn't just do that to us after all the practicing we had done.

We were so into our conversation that before we knew it we had been riding for an hour and had come to a dead end on the path with a brushy forest in front of us. We decided

it was time to take a break so we tied up our
horses and pushed the branches out of the
way so we could easily walk into the trees.
What we discovered was beautiful. There was
a meadow full of daisies outlined by the forest,
like when you outline colored pencil with
marker. It looked like a picture and just looking
at it seemed to calm us down and take our
mind off of the canceled show for a little while.

We realized that we hadn't told our parents where we were going and knew we'd better head back and let them know we were okay. As we walked back through the thick forest to get our horses, we heard a lot of spooky sounds all around us. Suddenly we were all scared out of our minds. We saw the bushes swaying and heard the crackling leaves under our boots. But some of the crackling wasn't because of us and when we heard it, we froze in place. We saw the bushes sway again.

Then it hit us, literally. It jumped out so fast we didn't even see what it was. It just jumped out at us and made us scream and squeal and run for our lives and then it disappeared into the trees.

We quickly got out of there, ran to our horses, untied them, and galloped off. We had a few scratches and scrapes from the prickly bushes, but other than that we were fine. As we quickly rode away, we looked back and all started to laugh uncontrollably as we saw the hideous monster coming out of the woods and following us. It was a gray house cat. We all felt really silly but glad that it wasn't anything truly hideous.

When we got back to the stables, our mothers were waiting for us and they didn't look totally happy that we had been gone so long. But we hurriedly told them the whole story and they said we did the right thing and that we were very brave, but we could see that they were trying not to laugh.

We all went back to the hotel together. In all the excitement and silliness, we had totally forgotten the horrific news about the judge, but after watching a sad movie it hit us and we cried ourselves to sleep.

*Exhausted, I slept really hard,* and when I woke up, I wondered, *Why are we still here? Wasn't the show yesterday? Aren't we leaving today?* I suddenly felt sad all over again.

I pulled on my favorite pink zebra-striped shirt and some Capri's. I looked through my stuff, found my diary, and flipped to a page that just so happened to be yesterday's entry, so I read it.

> Dear Diary,
> I just heard the bad news from my mother. The show has been canceled because one of the judges died. I feel really bad for his family but I have to do something, anything. I have been waiting for this moment forever.
> Sincerely,
> Sad Ellie

So the show didn't go on. *If the show didn't go on yesterday, or today, will it ever?*

Mom and Dad weren't quite ready to go yet and Miracle was still in the stables so I still had some time to figure out what to do. As I ran down to the stables, a plan came into my mind. I quickly saddled up Miracle and headed over to the arena and the judges' trailer that was nearby. I could hear voices inside so I knew someone was still there. I banged on the door and yelled, "Open up! Please! I want to ask you something."

One of the judges opened the door and let me in. "Can I help you" he asked. I looked at him for a few minutes as I tried to think of what to say. Finally I just blurted it out, "Why is the show canceled just because one judge has died? Can't you just get a new one? I was looking forward to the show, we all were. This is my life-long dream, but now it's ruined," I sputtered the words as tears started falling down my cheeks.

I could hear the judges' voices but the words weren't getting into my brain. I just stood there as they told me that the show was definitely canceled. I pleaded, but it didn't work. The show would not go on.

Five minutes later I stepped outside, crying my eyes out. *Why have they done this to me? It seems like nobody likes me anymore,* I thought pitifully. I hopped back on my Miracle and decided to ride all the way home to Cumming. I knew my parents would be mad and it would be a long ride, but I needed to think.

I pulled my cell phone out of my pocket and called Sandra. She didn't answer so I left a message saying, "Hey, it's Ellie. If you're wondering where I am, then here it is. I became very upset and decided to ride home to Cumming, so, bye."

*So that's all?* I thought. *This will be a great story to tell my own kids one day.*

It was a good plan but I didn't get very far before Mom and Dad pulled up next to me with the horse trailer behind the car. They had been frantic with worry when Sandra told them about my message!  Even though my dad was mad, they were relieved to find me.

My mother scolded me "Don't you ever do anything like that again!"as she hugged me and we put Miracle into the trailer and headed home. As you can imagine, I was grounded for forever.

When we got home and after taking care of Miracle, I checked my email (even though I wasn't technically supposed to because I was grounded). But I was glad I did because I had one message that was a really big relief to me. It wasn't long but it was all I needed to read. It said:

*Hey, Ellie, how are you? I thought about what you said, and I wanted to tell you that I understand. Even though the show still isn't going to go on, I thought you would like to know that it was okay to ask. I know every girl wants to hear that they are right. Am I right?*

*Your friend,*
*Judge John Smith*

I liked that email, and the judge was

definitely right about me wanting to hear I was right. I was still pretty sad that the show was canceled, even though I know we don't always get what we want. But this was different; this was a life-long dream. I couldn't just let go of a life-long dream!

I quickly called Sandra and Felicity and told them to meet me at the barn right away. When they got there I said, "Sandra, Felicity, saddle up! We are going back and we are going to make them do the show." I didn't have a plan yet, but I knew I had to get back to the arena.

"What? No! Jinx," they both said at the same time.

We saddled up our horses and made sure we had everything we would need. We traveled along the back roads and the whole way there I couldn't stop smiling because I was thinking that this was the right thing to do and that I was going to be a hero. I kept thinking that everybody would be proud of me, that we were going to save the day.

Then I looked at Felicity and Sandra and they seemed to be thinking, *Uh oh. We shouldn't have gone along with this. This isn't right. Our parents are going to be sooo mad.*

"Uh, I think we are going the wrong way. We should turn back," Sandra said in a very frightened voice.

I said, "Don't be such scaredy-cats. Have fun while you can." *They are still acting like little girls. It's time to teach them to have fun.* But even though I wouldn't admit it, I felt a little scared myself.

We finally arrived back at the stables, got our horses settled into the stalls that they had left not that many hours ago and then went back to the hotel. Boy was I happy.

I remembered Mom saying that we had paid for a couple more days so we were still booked in our hotel room and in her hurry to find me she had forgotten to turn in the keys.

I still had mine in my pocket so getting back into the room was easy.

In fact everything was going really well until my cell phone rang and I remembered that Mom had no idea about this little plan of mine. Big trouble equals ME.

# Chapter 4

I knew I was going to be in big trouble so I let the call go to voicemail as we tried to figure out what to do about the horse show. I figured Mom would be upset at first, but she'd get over it because she would be so relieved to find us.

Since we were there, we decided to go back to the arena to try to find the judges or someone we could talk into putting the show back on, but they were all gone. There was nothing more we could do until we came up with another plan so we went back to the hotel. We had left so quickly that we didn't have any luggage with us so we didn't have to worry about unpacking.

Back at home, Mom was worried when I didn't come down for dinner. She called Sandra's and Felicity's mothers and when they discovered that our horses were gone, they decided that we had gone for a horseback ride. When nighttime came and we hadn't returned, they knew something else was going on. At first they started to panic and then Mom and Dad  remembered how upset I was about the canceled horse show and how I had gotten on Miracle to ride all the way back home.  *Ellie would never try to ride Miracle back to Atlanta and she wouldn't just leave without telling us. Or would she?*

At the hotel we decided to get some rest, but I couldn't fall asleep and when I did, I slept horribly. I tossed and turned all night and woke up five different times. At one point I fell off the bed and woke up with a huge bump on the top of my head.

Finally I decided to walk down the hall to the vending machine to get a Coke and as I did I heard music coming from somewhere in the hotel. I'm just naturally curious so I had to find out where it was coming from. I took the elevator down to the lobby and as I stepped out of the elevator I saw people in the lobby, the arcade, and even the snack room.

I raced back up to our room, woke up Felicity and Sandra and we joined the party in the arcade playing Pac-Man and pinball. Finally we were all so tired that we just went back to our rooms, fell into bed and were quickly sound asleep.

In the meantime, Mom was driving to get us. When she arrived, she found us sound asleep after an exhausting night. Remember how I said I thought she wouldn't be mad? I was very wrong. Mom got so angry she was like a monkey who had his banana taken away. She brought all three of us home and grounded me again, immediately. Sandra and

Felicity were grounded too. I was grounded from T.V., computer, playing with friends, and, worst of all, Miracle for five weeks. I thought, *I guess I'll survive the whole five weeks.*

Who was I kidding? I could never survive five weeks without my Miracle.

# Chapter 5

Turns out I did survive the five weeks, but just barely. I still had one problem: What about the show? I came up with several ideas, but none of them worked for Mom. They either involved violence or they were just not practical. Sigh. What was I going to do? I couldn't just 'not do' the show, but I couldn't think of anything to convince the judges to actually do it either. Then all of a sudden a brilliant idea popped into my head.

I would email all the girls who were invited to the show. Together we could think of something. We were sure to find a way. But how was I going to find out who all the girls were and how would I get them all together? I wasn't sure, but I did know one thing: I was going to ask Mom first. I remembered what happened last time.

Mom suggested we call them, but we couldn't find their phone numbers. Then I remembered the email from Robin. I thought their email addresses might be on the invite. I checked, and sure enough they were.

*"To: Felicity, Sandra, Hannah, Rachel, Ellie, Jessica, Erin, Mary, Lola, Summer, Tatum, Sherry, Sharon, Victoria, Brooke, Ava, Faith, Morgan, Kimberly, Shelly, Amanda, Chloe, Abby, Andi, and Isabelle..."*

Beside each girl's name was her email address. I asked Mom if I could have twenty-five girls over for the weekend. I had to explain a little, but I was capable of doing that. All I

had to say was that it was for the horse show.
She understood why I was trying so hard,
and that I wouldn't give up until I got what I
wanted.

Mom agreed but on the condition that
some of the girls slept in the guest room, some
in my room, and some in the family room. I
emailed each girl and most of them replied
instantly. Others replied a few hours later, and
they all replied by the end of the day. They
came over late in the afternoon on Friday and
we figured out where everyone was sleeping.
We had nine people in the family room, eight
in my room, and eight in the guest room. It
was super crowded, but they all came.

I had made a fun plan for the night.
Slumber parties are the best time for pranks. I
told Felicity and Sandra about it, and they said
"Of course!"

First we sat in a circle and did each other's
toe nails and finger nails. We did them all the
same, with horses on the big toe. After that we

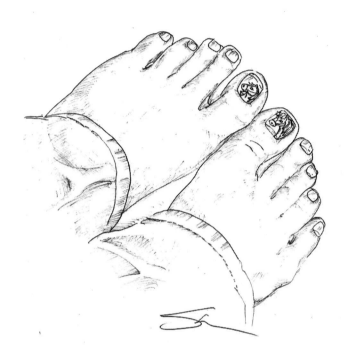

talked and watched movies. Finally we all went off to bed.

In the morning when the other girls sleeping in my room woke up, Sandra, Felicity, and I laughed because they were all drizzled with honey. Guilty as charged.

After they washed off and we woke up the girls who were sleeping in the other rooms and we gathered in the kitchen for breakfast, I said, "OK. Let's get to the point. The state equestrian show was canceled, but I want to get it back on the road, and I need your help. Ready or not, here we come. Right girls? Now, anyone have any ideas?"

The room was absolutely quiet except for the sounds Mom made while she prepared breakfast. Then a girl named Brooke slowly raised her hand into the air. I pointed to her, and she quickly said, "We could do a protest outside the arena."

I nodded, thinking of how that could work. It could work in many ways, and I thought we should do it. We needed to do anything we could. So, we spent the morning making our plans. Our biggest problem was when would we find all of the judges together at the arena? Mom overheard us talking and said that they were all there today because of a special event that was going on. Yea! Yea! Yea!

We asked Mom to drive us to Atlanta to the

judges' trailer. We also convinced four other moms to drive their SUVs, so we would all fit.

We quickly made our signs and figured out our plan. We all piled into the vehicles a little after lunch. OMG were we excited! We just knew this would work! I was a genius! I would get my life-long dream. I just knew it.

When we got to the arena, we parked, got our signs out, and got ready to go. Our moms weren't sure it would work, but I was. We stood in front of the door to the judges' trailer, and the judges stepped out, chuckling.

Right then we started chanting, "Get the show on the road. Get the show on the road." After awhile we stopped and stood in a straight line, waiting patiently for an answer.

My mom was thinking all along that there was no way this could work, but like a loving Mom, she let me try. I should have listened to her. When we stopped, the judges smiled and started chanting, "No, no, no. But we do like your persistence."

We all looked at each other, walked back to the cars and quietly climbed in. It was silent the whole way home. Everyone was upset. I thought *I shouldn't have gotten them into this. It's my fault that they are upset. I should have just gone with Felicity and Sandra. Then only three girls would have been upset.* I felt so guilty.

What did we have to do to get the judges to agree to hold the show? Every single time we asked, the answer was no. I didn't understand it. Was this about more than the judge who died? I just couldn't figure it out.

Then I thought, *I will keep trying. They can ruin my dream, but they will never, ever destroy my spirit and love for horses. No one will. It's impossible to destroy my spirit and love for horses. I hope that is the same with my dream.*

# Chapter 6

Since we had a break from school, our moms agreed that all twenty-five girls could stay at our house for the next week, giving us time to discuss some more things we could do. Brooke had the most ideas, but the best words came from Summer. It wasn't an actual idea but what she said made me feel good. She said, "No matter what, we are going to do the show."

I already believed that but it felt good to hear it from someone else and just hearing those words gave me another idea.

"You know what?" I said, "I don't care if we

have judges or not, I am doing the show. No matter what anyone says or does, I am doing the show. I don't care if everyone in the world tries to stop me, it still won't demolish my dream. Nothing will. I will keep trying. "

I didn't know what to do or what to say. It was just so hard having so many people depend on me. I felt like I had the world resting on my shoulders. I was trying to find my way through the problem, but I felt like I was trying to find a needle in a haystack. I couldn't be held under this much pressure. Then it hit me.

"Wait! What I said before, about doing the show with or without the judges. That's the idea: Do the show without the judges. At least, without those judges! We can ask our parents to find new judges. People we don't know, so it will be fair and square."

I ran down the stairs and said, "Mom, do you know anyone who could act as a judge for the horse show?"

"Not really, why?" So I told mom my idea

and as she listened, she began to agree that it could work as she thought of people who would be able to act as judges. I was so excited I ran back upstairs to my room to tell everyone. By the time I got there, my legs were tired. I let them repose for a moment and I rested on my bed. Then, I fell asleep so hard no one could wake me up. It was really exhausting being in charge!

While I slept, Sandra, Felicity, and Mom called three of Mom's suggestions and asked them if they would judge our show. They all said yes! What a relief! We had one less thing to figure out. We were almost there, almost ready to do the show.

Even though we had crossed that hurdle, I was worried that this might not work. But I cheered myself up by thinking, *you never know, it might.* Yet there were still other hurdles to jump. The other competitors' parents might say no or we might not be able to get access to the arena. I knew those were a couple of ways it could be ruined. But it had to work. I didn't think this group of ours could think of any more ideas.

Even though we now had judges, we still had a lot to figure out, like how to hold the show and if we were able to. Using our best puppy-dog faces we all asked my mom to help yet again. She fell for it and said, "Well, okay, but only this last time." Even though I knew she would help whenever we needed it. That was just how my mom was.

"YEA! Finally, we get to do the show!" We cheered.

Wait. There was one more thing. We had to tell the national organization about this. We had to get their permission. So, we had to ask Mom to help again and then we had to beg and she said yes, but only if we stopped begging. So we stopped begging and waited quietly just looking at her with our sad faces. She tried not to smile, but finally she did and agreed to ask some of the other Moms to help drive us to the national organization's headquarters in another state. OMG, I couldn't believe our Moms were really going to help us do this! Our problems were almost solved! We all fell asleep easily that night.

The next morning we woke up and felt stress free. It was almost like a magical fairy came by and dropped stress-free dust on all of us. We washed up, packed our bags, and changed into our prettiest clothes. Then it was time to go. Since we were in different cars, we kept connected by phone. One person would call someone in the second car then that person would call someone in the third car, and then the fourth car... Then we all just talked and giggled.

It was a long road trip and took more than a day. When we finally arrived at a hotel we fell asleep almost immediately, excited about what the next day would bring.

When we arrived at the national headquarters the next day, at first we just ran around looking at where we might be when we competed in the nationals. We completely forgot about what we had to do first until Mom said, "Okay, girls. I thought this was business. Let's get to it. Chop, chop, in other words."

So we walked around trying to find someone who worked there who could help us. We found a trainer, but she was no help. After that we bumped into Robin Whayhuter! She saw me and realized that she recognized me.

"What are you doing here?" she asked.

I replied with a simple but sophisticated, "Well, we are trying to find the headquarters so we can get the state show going, or else they won't have enough entries for nationals. And we all know how _that_ turns out."

She said, "Well to start off, the headquarters' office is right in that building over there and..."

We ran to the building she had pointed to and pushed the doors open.

"Okay go ahead, I had nothing else to say," we heard her say.

After a few minutes of searching and more asking, we found the director of the organization. He seemed surprised to see twenty-five girls crowding into his office as I stepped forward and said, "Hi, I am Ellie and our state show has been canceled. We'd all like to compete, so we were curious. Can we run our own show? If we don't, you won't have enough people for nationals. Please?"

As we were waiting for an answer, Robin walked in the door and asked the director if she could talk with him in private. They kicked us out of the office and closed the door. We tried to hear what they were saying but it was all muffled – we couldn't make out the words.

Finally the office door opened. We all crossed our fingers as the director watched us for a few minutes. Finally after what seemed like forever, he said, "Yes."

The room was totally silent. Even though it was what we wanted to hear, it wasn't what we had expected. I was so excited I just blurted out, "That's all you are going to say? Just yes, that's all? Wait. You said 'yes!' Thank you, thank you, thank you! I guess we better go get to work. Bye."

Our Moms stayed behind to talk to Robin and the director to get all the details of what had to be done, but we had gotten what we wanted. All twenty-five of us girls went racing outside where we could yell and jump and celebrate.

# Chapter 7

We were so clever. I knew never giving up would pay off. I was so delighted that the national organization would let us do our own show. I knew that if the state show didn't go on they wouldn't have enough competitors for nationals. Then the world show might have to be canceled, too. So, in a way, they were lucky to have us. I felt like such a hero. I was so pumped, I decided to write about it in my diary. Every day I would write a little more.

Dear Diary,

I am so happy that I am able to reach my goal. I feel so fascinated, like I'm floating on air. I can see everyone around me so proud of me, like I just saved a little baby from getting hit by a car. I can feel my heart pumping out of my chest.

Happy Ellie

That was a good start; I'd write more later because right now there was a lot to do.

Our Moms were handling the details and all my friends were already packing everything in sight, partly because they were leaving to go back to their own homes, but mostly because they were so excited about going to the show and they needed something to do. They even got a little carried away and started packing my stuff! "Okay, girls, don't pack my stuff. Girls, hey! Put that down. That's fragile. GIRLS!"

They all looked at me with scared faces, and dropped anything and everything in their hands. Then we all laughed. It was like I was the leader of England and everyone bowed at my feet. It kind of felt cool.

As I watched them pack I thought of something: We had to celebrate our accomplishments. But how? We needed something fun, close, and easy and since all of the girls were leaving in the morning we needed to celebrate today. Then I had an idea! Perfect, perfect and perfect—a pool party.

The weather was unseasonably warm for the spring (but I do live in Georgia!) and I have a pool. So having a pool party is fun, and it's easy. I invited all of my school friends, and when they arrived that afternoon, we put on our bathing suits, got our towels, and ran downstairs. We had a contest to see who could get in the pool first by doing a cannon ball. Ava won! She's fast and furious.

It had been a while since I had spent any

time with my friends from school and they got along with the girls from the horse show, it was great! We swam and played volleyball and basketball. We had some races, too. We played lots of sports and games. It was a blast!

After swimming, my school friends had to go home and Mom called me and my horse show friends in for dinner. We had roast beef, potatoes, and corn. It was a big meal because the other girls were leaving the next day. We were all hungry and we all eat like horses!

After dinner we took turns showering and then we watched scary movies. When we got too freaked out we decided to watch comedies instead. That was fun, but eventually we had to go to bed. We all had nightmares about the same movie. It was the scariest movie of them all.

Early in the morning we woke up and shuffled downstairs. I was halfway down when I smelled pancakes or waffles; I wasn't sure which one. It was both! I was in the lap of luxury. The only thing that could make it better was having all the girls stay with us forever. But I knew that wasn't going to happen. So I settled on the pancakes and waffles.

One by one the Moms came and picked them up. To every girl I said, "Bye! It was nice having you stay here. See you at the show."

I had to say that twenty-five times. I was upset they all had to leave, but I would see them again in a short while at our horse show.

# Chapter 8

Time seemed to drag and the competition felt like it was taking forever to get here. But soon I realized, *In a few days I can say that my dream is accomplished.*

If only it could come quicker! I wondered if I went to sleep for a while, whether the day would go by faster, so I tried it. I flopped on the living room couch and turned on the TV because I fall asleep faster if the TV is on. It worked! I fell fast asleep. I slept through dinner and the whole night and still woke up later than everyone else the next day. *So it's true*, I thought, *the day does go faster if you sleep.*

Then it was finally the day we had to pack for our week-long trip. I made a list of everything that I had to have and some little extras.

1) 8 t-shirts
2) 8 shorts
3) 3 jeans
4) 3 socks
5) *New Moon* (book)
6) Nintendo DS
7) All my riding gear
8) Money
9) Great-Grandma's ring

My handwriting was messy but only because I quickly jotted everything down. That was everything I needed. Then I picked out all of my favorite clothes, got my zebra-print suitcase out of the closet and plopped everything into it. In five-to-ten minutes I had everything on my list scratched out and packed.

Tomorrow was finally the day we were leaving for the state show. I was so pumped that I did my little hooray dance. I ran down the stairs and stopped at the third step, where I jumped off and yelled, "Yippee ki-yea!"

My mom told me to stop fooling around and just eat dinner. I did and then I sat in bed watching TV all night. Well, really only until 10:00 p.m. Then I fell asleep and dreamt of the show.

As soon as I woke up I ran to my parent's room and said, "Get up! It's time to go." They shushed me and whispered for me to go get dressed and put my stuff in the car. I did exactly what they said.

Finally the car roared out of the driveway. By the time we arrived at the hotel, the other girls had too.

"Hey, girls! I am so glad to see you here. Let's hope the show doesn't get canceled again. Ha!" I giggled at my own humor.

We walked up to our room and unpacked

all our stuff. Felicity, Sandra, and I wandered around the hotel. We knew where everything was since we had been there a few times before. We played arcade games with the other girls, but then my back started to ache, so I went back up to our room and laid on the bed and rested. The day was over, but the competition was just beginning.

The next morning was our first practice day. I had the same pattern to memorize and perform, so all I had to do was practice it again and again and again. The next day was another practice day, and so were the two days after that.

The fifth day was different, because we had to clean our stalls and get our horses ready. I did a lot of work with my horse. To start off, I cleaned out her stall. Next I washed Miracle, cleaned out her hooves, curried her, and braided her mane and tail. Then I went back to the hotel to get myself ready for the show. This time it was going to go on, and I was sure of it.

Since sleeping passes the time, I went to bed.

I woke up feeling like the greatest person in the world—like anything could happen at that moment. I was thinking, *Today is the show and it isn't going be canceled again. I am going down there right now to make sure of it.*

So I ran down to the arena and asked, "It is still going on, right?"

The new judges nodded.

I got ready just in time. My number was 5667. The show started and there were two rounds—racing and jumping. The judges called number 5665, so I knew I was going to be on soon. Before I knew it, the judges announced numbers 5666 and 5667. That was me! I trotted through the wrought-iron gates and did my jumping pattern. It felt glorious!!

But as we continued to do our pattern I mixed them up! Dang it! How could I after all my practice! So now I was ranked seventh, and I had to get up to fifth. Felicity was fifth and

Sandra was third. I still had one more round.
Everyone did their jumping routine perfectly
except for me. I was really bummed.

   Now it was time for the racing. Five people
at a time race each other. I raced Ava, Faith,

Brooke, and Lola. I got fourth; I thought that might move me up.

Turns out it moved me up to sixth place, but I still wasn't proceeding to the national show. After all that, I wasn't going to get my life-long dream! At first I was really bummed but then I looked on the bright side—Felicity and Sandra DID make it to the national show.

# Chapter 9

We walked out of the arena with the reins in our hands and our horses standing proudly next to us. I was glad I placed sixth, but I knew I could have done better. Felicity and Sandra received ribbons, a yellow and a green. I received NONE. I really felt I should have at least received one for participation, but no!

We walked into the stable and clipped our horses to the sides of the wash station so they wouldn't go anywhere. We looked through the grooming bucket and found a brush to bring all the dirt to the top of our horse's coat. Finally we brushed their manes and tails, picked out their dirty hooves, washed the horses off with a hose, and dried them off.

We took our horses to the trailer and walked them in, hopped in the back seat and Dad started to drive us home. We were all pretty quiet. I think Sandra and Felicity were afraid that I was really upset; I wasn't sure what I was feeling, so I just didn't feel like talking.

When we were about halfway home we stopped to eat at a Cracker Barrel restaurant. I had never been there before. I guess there is a first time for everything. In a weird way, that made me happy because I knew that I still had a lot of first times ahead of me.

We drove the rest of the way home. It felt like two seconds and we were there. When Felicity's dad came to pick up her and Sandra, Mom asked if we wanted to play our favorite game that we often play when we get home from a trip, Capture the Flag. My team always wins. The teams were my mom, my dad, and Felicity's dad versus Felicity, Sandra, and me. We knew exactly where they hid their flag; we just had to get over there without them tagging us. The game was really fun and it took my mind off the competition and that I hadn't placed. I think my Mom knew I needed that.

My team tagged two of the other team, so they were in jail. We had one person guard the jail and two people go over to their side. They only had one person left—Mom—and she cannot tag two people at the same time! I distracted her while Sandra grabbed the flag. I felt powerful again! I was good at winning!

A few days later Sandra and Felicity were at my house again and we were watching some movies. We weren't talking much about the show and I wasn't asking them about the national competition or when it was. I wanted to know…but then I didn't.

We got tired of watching movies and

decided to check our emails. I checked first and I had received three emails, one of them had the subject of "State participation."

The email said…
*Thank you for participating in the state equestrian show. We are proud of your performance and are sorry that you will not be going to the national competition.*

*We wish you the best of luck for next year.*

*Sincerely,*
*Your friends at the National Equestrian Organization.*

*That was very sweet of them* I thought even though I would rather the note had said I did make it to the national show. Bummer!

Then Felicity checked her email and screamed, "Yea! I am going to the national show. Sandra, the email was sent to you, too."

I sat there silently for a moment, waiting for them to say something. They did, but not too much. I felt like a fifth wheel, or in this case, the third. I walked out of the room with tears welling up in my eyes. They followed me with glorious grins on their faces, like they had just won the lottery. They had and I hadn't.

My mom knew exactly why I was upset but I didn't think Sandra and Felicity even noticed, they were just so excited for themselves.

Then Sandra said, "Hey, Ellie, you should come with us to the national show."

My back was facing them but when I heard that I turned around fast as a roller coaster.

"Really?" I asked.

They nodded almost like they were smiling through their teeth, but they weren't. I really was happy for them. I ran over to the fridge and grabbed a bottle of Gatorade and drank it all in about ten seconds. This was the happiest moment of my life, them going to the national show and me going with them. Nothing could top this.

I felt much better. Together we walked to my room and sat on the bed. For the first five minutes we just sat there looking at each other. Then I got a conversation going.

"So, guys, are you ready for the show? Do you know when and where it is?"

They replied with a crooked look on their face, "Uh, no, no, and no. We aren't ready at all. I guess you could say we don't know what we got ourselves into."

As we talked I thought about being friends. We don't turn against each other. They accomplished something good—going to the national horse show. I knew that, and I was happy for them. As Mom says, "To have a friend, you have to be a friend." So I would be a good friend and celebrate their accomplishments.

I know we will stay friends until the very moment that we die. We will never break apart. We do everything together now and that is how it will stay—together forever always.